Essential Fiction
Anthology

COMPILED BY

Brian Moses

D1335672

Heinemann

Contents

stories with familiar settings

~ **The Twelfth Floor Kids**   4
by Ruth Symes

~ **It's Not Fair! … that I'm little**   6
by Bel Mooney

poetry based on observation and the senses

~ **Bed in Summer**   10
by Robert Louis Stevenson

~ **Listen**   11
by Tony Langham

traditional story

~ **Rumpelstiltskin**   12
retold by Dee Reid

story with familiar setting

~ **The Tasting Game**   18
by Paul Stewart

shape poetry

~ **Ten Ways to Travel**   22
by Penny Kent

~ **The River**   23
by James Carter

parables

~ **The Gifts at the Bottom of the Well**   24
traditional

~ **The Crowded House**   26
retold by Robin Fisher

fables

~ **The Dog and the Bone**   28
retold by Hiawyn Oram

~ **The Stag and his Spindly Legs**   29
retold by Hiawyn Oram

oral and performance poetry from different cultures

~ **If You Want To See An Alligator**   30
by Grace Nichols

Fisherman Chant   31
by John Agard

myth	~	**Birth of the Stars** *retold by James Riordan*	32
legend	~	**Baíra and the Vultures Who Owned Fire** *retold by Sean Taylor*	34
oral and performance poetry from different cultures	~	**Gran, Can You Rap?** *by Jack Ousbey*	38
	~	**The Travellin' Britain Rap** *by Wes Magee*	40
adventure story	~	**The Toad Tunnel** *by Anthony Masters*	42
poetry that plays with language	~	**How Can I?** *by Brian Moses*	46
	~	**At the End of School Assembly** *by Simon Pitt*	47
riddle	~	**A Riddle** *by Tony Bradman*	48
poetry that plays with language	~	**My Dad's Amazing!** *by Ian Souter*	49
stories by the same author	~	**The Hodgeheg** *by Dick King-Smith*	50
	~	**King Max The Last** *by Dick King-Smith*	54
adventure story	~	**Stranded!** *by Andrew Collett*	58
humorous poetry	~	**Through the Staffroom Door** *by Brian Moses*	62
	~	**Recipe for a Disastrous Family Picnic** *by Ian Souter*	63

The Twelfth Floor Kids

Ruth Symes

This is Beechtree Flats. The twelfth-floor kids live high up on the twelfth floor. Their names are Amy, Dan, Seeta and Eddie.

Meet Amy

Hi, my name's Amy. I live on the twelfth floor of Beechtree Flats with my mum and dad, my twin baby brothers, Nicky and James, and my big sister, Tina.

This is my room. This is a poster of Red Fox.

Meet Eddie

Hi, I'm Eddie. I live in this flat with my mum and big sister, Jess.

Mum and Jess work in Mum's shop in the High Street. Sometimes I start to make the dinner for when they get home.

I've always lived in this flat. I like looking over the balcony and seeing what's happening far down below.

Meet Seeta

Hello, I'm Seeta. I live here with my dad and mum and two older brothers.

This is my room. I like doing magic tricks and when I grow up I'm going to be a magician. This is my jar of starry stuff. I bought it at the art shop. It's a special sort of paint that glitters when it dries.

Meet Dan

Hi, my name's Dan. I live with Mum and my cat, Jinny. My dad lives over the other side of town and sometimes I go to see him at the weekend.

I've had Jinny ever since she was a kitten. When I go to bed Jinny curls up and goes to sleep at the end of my bed.

Meet Jinny

'Miaow.'

Illustrated by Nick Ward

It's Not Fair! ... that I'm little

Bel Mooney

Kitty was the smallest girl in her class. Usually she did not care. She could swim well, and run as fast as most people – well, almost – and once came first in the egg-and-spoon race on Sports Day. So it did not matter – being small. That was what Kitty thought.

But one day something happened to make her change her mind. It was one of those days when nothing went right.

First of all, there was a new boy in Kitty's class. His name was Tom, and he was very, very tall. Kitty didn't like him very much, because he called her 'Shrimp'. The whole class was working on a mural in paint and cut-out paper, and on this day Kitty and Tom and two other children were chosen to do special extra work on it.

Kitty was very excited. She loved painting – especially when you could be really messy. That was why she wanted to paint the sky, with lovely big fluffy clouds floating along. But each time she tried Tom laughed at her.

'You can't reach,' he said. 'You're too small.' And he leaned over her head, and did the bit she wanted to do.

At break she found someone had put her jacket on one of the higher pegs she could not reach and she wouldn't ask Tom or anyone to get it down. So she went outside without it and felt cold. Then the playground helper told her off for not wearing a coat.

'I couldn't reach it,' said Kitty in a small voice.

'Oh, you're such a dear little thing,' said the lady nicely.

Kitty sighed. It really was not fair.

Then it was the games lesson, when the girls had to play netball. They were learning to stop each other getting the ball. You had to dodge quickly, and jump very high. Kitty wasn't very good at that.

Today she was worse than ever. She did not get hold of the ball once. All of the other girls had longer arms and legs and it seemed easy for them. Afterwards one of the girls said something that hurt Kitty very much. 'No one will want you in their team, Kitty. You're too tiny!'

7

Kitty was very quiet when she got home. Her mum noticed. At last Kitty broke into tears. 'It's not fair that I'm little,' she sobbed.

Kitty told her mum everything. Mum nodded. 'It isn't easy. I was small when I was a little girl, and you ask Daniel what they say to him in school.'

Surprised, Kitty went to find her big brother to ask him. He made a face. 'They sometimes call me Shorty,' he said. 'But it's very friendly, so I don't mind.'

'Are you small too?' asked Kitty.

'Yes. But I'd rather be me than the boy in our class who's so tall and thin they call him Stringy!'

'You see,' said Mum, 'most people have got something about themselves they would like to change. When you know that, it makes you feel better about yourself.'

Kitty thought about that and she made a plan. The next day, at playtime, she made herself feel brave enough to go up to Tom when he was standing on his own.

'Tom, can I ask you something?' she said.

'What, Shrimp?'

'If you had one wish, what would you change about yourself?'

The tall boy looked surprised. Then he went pink and whispered, 'My hair. I hate my hair.' Kitty looked at it. It was orangey-brown. She thought it was rather nice.

70 'At my old school they called me Carrots,' he said, 'and it wasn't fair. But don't you tell anyone, will you – Shrimp?'

Kitty said she wouldn't.

Then she found Susie, the big strong girl who had said Kitty was no good at netball, and asked her the same question. Susie frowned and answered quickly.

'My size,' she said, 'because I feel like an elephant. I'd like to be smaller. I'd like to be like you.'

'Like me?' squeaked Kitty, amazed.

80 Susie nodded.

Kitty looked round the playground at all the children running around. Some tall, some small. Some fat, some thin. Some dark, some fair. Some shy, some bold. Some who could sing, some who could swim. Some dainty, some clumsy ...

'We're all different,' she said to herself, 'and I suppose that's fair!'

Illustrated by Nick Schon

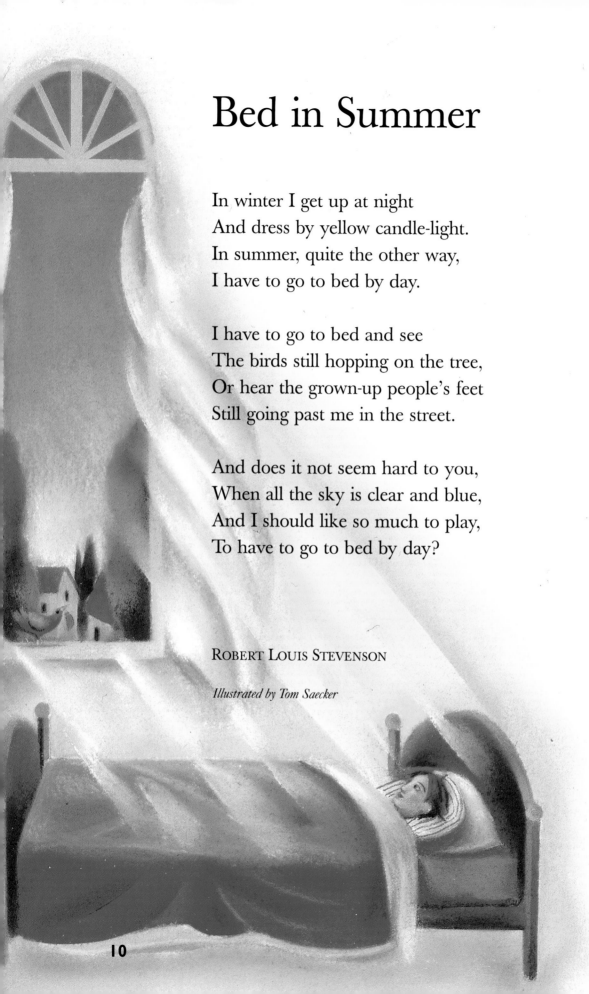

Bed in Summer

In winter I get up at night
And dress by yellow candle-light.
In summer, quite the other way,
I have to go to bed by day.

I have to go to bed and see
The birds still hopping on the tree,
Or hear the grown-up people's feet
Still going past me in the street.

And does it not seem hard to you,
When all the sky is clear and blue,
And I should like so much to play,
To have to go to bed by day?

ROBERT LOUIS STEVENSON

Illustrated by Tom Saecker

Listen

Listen!
(What can you hear?)
The crashing waves
of a distant sea,
A faraway bird
calling to me ...

Listen!
(What can you hear?)
The buzz-buzz buzzing
of a bumble bee,
The sound of the wind
in a sycamore tree ...

Listen!
(What can you hear?)
The rattle and roar
of an express train,
The sound of rain-drops
on a window pane ...

Listen!
(What can you hear?)
The pitter-patter
of the paws of a mouse,
A creaking door
in a spooky old house ...

Listen!
(What can you hear?)
The hoot of an owl
in the still of the night,
The sigh of flowers
opening in sunlight ...

Listen!
(What can you hear?)
Listen!
(What can ...)
Sshhh! Don't say a thing.
Listen!
(What can you hear?)

... everything.

Tony Langham

Illustrated by Tom Saecker

Rumpelstiltskin

RETOLD BY DEE REID

Once upon a time there was a poor miller who loved to boast about his beautiful daughter. One day, the miller went to see the King. 'Sire,' he said, 'my daughter is so clever, she can even spin straw into gold.'

Now the King was very fond of gold and he said to the miller, 'Let's see if your daughter really can spin straw into gold.'

At once the miller regretted his foolish words but it was too late. The King led the miller's daughter to a room full of straw.

'Now we'll see how clever you are,' said the King. 'Spin all this straw into gold before morning or I'll chop off your head.'

When the King had left, the poor girl began to cry. She couldn't spin straw into gold. Suddenly the door burst open and a strange little man appeared.

'Why are you crying?' he asked.

'I must spin this straw into gold or the King will chop off my head,' said the girl.

'What will you give me if I spin the straw into gold for you?' the little man asked.

'I will give you my necklace,' said the girl.

So the little man set to work. By morning all the straw had been spun into gold.

When the King saw the gold he was very pleased, but it made him even greedier, so that evening he put the poor girl into a larger room, with even more straw.

'Spin all this straw into gold before morning or I'll chop off your head,' said the King.

When the King had left, the girl began to cry. Suddenly the door burst open and the strange little man appeared again.

'What will you give me this time if I spin the straw into gold for you?' the little man asked.

'I'll give you my ring,' said the girl.

So the little man set to work. By morning all the straw had been spun into gold.

When the King saw the gold he was very pleased, but now he wanted even more gold, so that evening he put the poor girl into an *enormous* room full of straw.

This time the King said, 'If you spin all this straw into gold before morning, then I will marry you and you will be my Queen.'

Once again as soon as the King had left the strange little man appeared.

50

'This time I have no gift to give you,' said the girl sadly.

'If I help you,' he said, 'you must promise to give me your first-born child.'

The girl didn't know what else to do, so she agreed.

When the King saw all the gold he was very very pleased. So he married the girl, and she became Queen. A year later she had a beautiful baby daughter.

60   One day the Queen was in the nursery with her
daughter when the door burst open and there was
the strange little man.

'I have come for the baby,' he said. 'Remember
you promised that I could have your first-born child.'

The Queen began to cry. She begged the little
man not to take away her child. He felt sorry for her
so he said, 'I will give you three days. If in that time,
you can guess my name, you may keep your child.'

So the Queen lay awake all night thinking of
70   names. When the little man came the next day she
said, 'Is your name Sidney?'

'No!' said the little man.

'Is it Albert or Ernest?'

'No! No! You have not guessed my name,' said the
little man as he danced around the room.

The next day the miller visited his daughter and she begged him to help her save her baby. Together they thought of all the strangest names. When the little man came she said, 'Perhaps your name is Bandylegs, or Dribbledrub? Or Poddlewidden?'

'No! No! No!' laughed the little man. 'You have not guessed my name.'

Then the miller had an idea. He set out to look for the little man. He searched all day and was just about to give up when he saw a little house at the edge of the forest. The miller peeped in and saw the strange little man. He was dancing in front of the fire and he sang as he danced,

> *'Tonight I dance around this flame.*
> *Tomorrow a beautiful daughter I'll claim.*
> *And no one will ever guess my game*
> *For Rumpelstiltskin is my name!'*

The miller crept away from the cottage without saying a word.

The next morning the nursery door burst open and in came the strange little man.

'This is your last chance,' he said. 'What is my name?'

'Is it Herbert?' asked the Queen.

'No!' said the little man.

100 'Is it Humphrey?' asked the Queen.

'No!' said the little man. 'You will never guess my name.'

'Could it be possibly be RUMPELSTILTSKIN?' asked the Queen triumphantly.

The little man was furious. 'How did you find out?' he screamed and he stamped his foot so hard that it went right through the floor. This made him even more angry and he pulled at his leg so hard that he tore himself in two.

110 And that was the end of the strange little man.

Illustrated by Mik Brown

The Tasting Game

Paul Stewart

It was too wet to play out, so I decided to teach Ben the Tasting Game. I used to play it with Dad years ago – before Ben was even born.

'It's easy,' I said. 'You put on a blindfold. Then I give you something to taste and you tell me what it is. Then we swap round. See? The first one to get ten right, wins.'

Ben nodded, but then said, 'I want chocolate spread first.'

10 'I'll show you,' I laughed. I tied the scarf into place and pushed the spoon into his mouth.

'Strawberry jam,' Ben grinned.

'Yeah,' I said. 'One-nil!'

'Another go,' said Ben.

'It's my turn now,' I said.

Unable to see through the scarf, I heard Ben rummaging about in the cupboard. 'Careful not to spill anything,' I said. If there was any mess, I knew who'd get the blame.

20 'I *am* being caref— whoops!'

I tore off the blindfold. The floor was covered in sugar.

'You idiot!' I shouted.

'It was an accident!' Ben cried.

'It always is,' I muttered. But that wasn't how Mum and Dad would see it.

I cleaned everything up as best I could, and the game went on – cranberry jelly – peanut butter – some raisins – syrup.

30   The points built up, the floor grew stickier, but the game was going well. Then I tried Ben with some cheese.

'I want something else,' Ben pouted, and wouldn't take the blindfold off.

'Okay, then,' I said angrily. Younger brothers *always* have to have their way. 'Here's something else!' I pushed the spoon back in his mouth. Ben didn't react.

'So, what is it?' I said.

40   'Salt,' said Ben quietly. He removed the scarf. 'I don't want to play any more.'

I wasn't surprised. The thing about the Tasting Game is that you *have* to trust the other person, and I'd broken that trust. To win it back, I had to let Ben give me something horrible.

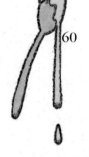

The vinegar was revolting, but could have been worse. Then it was Ben's turn again.

'Come on,' I said, holding the spoon to his mouth.

'What is it?' Ben asked suspiciously.

50 'Just open your mouth,' I said.

But he wouldn't, and as I stared at his tightly pursed lips, I started getting angry again. *Be* like that then, I thought. I flicked the ice-cream into the sink, and replaced it with mustard. Then I pinched Ben's nose, and shoved the spoon into his mouth.

This time, the effect was instant.

'That was mean and horrible!' he howled, and burst into tears.

I'd gone too far. I rushed to get him some orange 60 squash. 'Drink this,' I said. 'And don't cry!'

If he didn't stop soon, I knew I'd be in for it.

At that moment, Mum and Dad burst in. They looked at the mess all over the kitchen. They looked at us.

'What have you been doing?' they both shouted. Ben was still sobbing too loudly to speak.

'Well, Steve?' said Dad.

'We were playing the Tasting Game,' I explained. 'We ...'

70 Then Mum noticed the pot of mustard on the kitchen unit and they guessed the rest.

'But why?' said Dad.

Why? Because Ben didn't trust me. Because I wanted to see what would happen. Because I wanted to make him cry so that you'd shout 'Act your age' like you do with me ...

'Steve, I'm waiting!' Dad snapped.

I looked up into his angry face. 'I HATE BEING THE OLDEST!' I screamed, and found myself
80 blubbing as loudly as Ben.

I expected a smack or, at the very least, one of them to say that I was acting like a baby. What I didn't expect was what actually happened.

Dad crouched down, wrapped his arms round both me and Ben, and drew us towards him.

'My two little monsters,' he whispered.

The hug said the rest.

'Come on,' said Mum finally. 'Let's have one last round of the Tasting Game.'

90 Ben and I dried our eyes and went into the dining room. Dad tied the blindfolds. A moment later, Mum came in and I felt a glass being placed against my lips. Banana milkshake had never tasted so good!

Illustrated by Nick Sharratt

Ten Ways to Travel

hop   hop   hop   hop

hop   hop   hop   hop

bounce   bounce   bounce

tiptoe   tiptoe   tiptoe   tiptoe

roll over and over and over and over

wrigglewrigglewrigglewrigglewriggle

stroll   stroll

run run runrunrunrunrunrunrun leeeaaap

cartwheel cartwheel cartwheel cartwheel cartwheel

danced danced danced danced

sssspring ssspring sssspring

flop.

Penny Kent

22

The River

JAMES CARTER

from
a
  tiny
    spring
     the
      river
       came
        and
       wound
      its
     way
    for
   days
  and
 days
first
  east
then
west
but
  always
    south
     always
      down
     even
   when
  it
  c
  u
  r
  l
  e
  d
   itself
    a
    r
    o
    u
    n
   d
    a
   b
 e n
   d
   but
   then
  one day
 something changed
and a river it could no longer be

FOR THE RIVER GREW AND THE
RIVER KNEW THAT NOW IT WAS THE SEA THE SEA
THE SEA THE SEA THE SEA THE SEA THE SEA THE
SEA THE SEA THE SEA THE SEA THE SEA THE SEA
THE SEA THE SEA THE SEA THE SEA THE SEA THE
SEA THE SEA THE SEA THE SEA THE SEA THE SEA
THE SEA THE SEA THE SEA THE SEA THE SEA THE

The Gifts at the Bottom of the Well

A traditional Italian tale

Once there were two sisters. One was very good but the other was very naughty.

One day their mother said, 'Girls, please go and fetch some water from the well.'

The bad sister stamped her foot and said, 'No!' But the good sister ran off to the well at once.

She took a bucket, fixed it to the rope, and let it down the well. Suddenly the rope snapped – and the bucket went tumbling down to the bottom.

The good sister was worried that her mother would be angry with her for losing the bucket. So she climbed into the well to find it.

When she reached the bottom of the well, she had a surprise. There was no water!

She found herself in a long, dark passage with three doors. No one answered when she knocked at the first two doors. But the third door was answered by a smiling fairy who said, 'I have found your bucket. You can have it back, but first you must sweep my floor and then give my baby his dinner.'

The good sister went into the house and set to work. As she swept the floor, she found many sparkling jewels among the dust. She pulled them out carefully and gave them to the fairy. Then she prepared the baby's dinner. It smelt delicious but she didn't taste even the tiniest bit.

10

The fairy was pleased. 'Here's the bucket,' she said. 'When you come out of the well, look up at the sky.'

30 The girl climbed out of the well and looked up at the sky. A shining star fell on to her face and gave her the most beautiful smile.

She ran home. Her bad sister saw the beautiful smiling face and felt jealous. 'How did you get that?' she cried. The good sister told her about the fairy at the bottom of the well.

So the bad sister ran to the well and threw a bucket to the bottom. Then she climbed down after it. In the dark passage she knocked at each of the doors – one, two, three.

40 The third door was answered by the smiling fairy. 'I will give you back your bucket,' she said. 'But first you must do some jobs for me.'

The bad sister went into the fairy's house to sweep the floor and feed the baby.

She found the jewels among the dust on the floor. When the fairy wasn't looking, she filled her pockets with the sparkling jewels. Then she gobbled up most of the baby's dinner herself, so that the little one cried with hunger.

50 The fairy was not pleased, but gave the bucket back to her and said, 'When you come out of the well, look up at the sky.'

The bad sister climbed out of the well and looked up at the sky.

A horrid lump of dirt fell on her face and gave her an angry scowl.

And from that day on the bad sister's face was stuck with a horrible scowl while the good sister's face always shone with a beautiful smile.

Illustrated by Tony Ross

The Crowded House

A traditional Jewish tale

RETOLD BY ROBERT FISHER

There once lived a poor Jewish farmer named Yitzak who had a very large family, and lived in a very small hut. Yitzak's house was so crowded that his children had to take turns to sleep in one tiny bed.

At last Yitzak could stand it no longer. So he went to see the Rabbi to ask him what to do about his impossible situation.

The wise Rabbi thought hard and long and at last he had an idea.

10 'I will tell you what to do,' he said. 'Bring your chicken to live with you inside the house.'

Yitzak couldn't understand how the chicken would help, but he trusted the Rabbi's wisdom and did as he was told. But as soon as the chicken was inside the house it grew frightened and flapped around the room, scattering its feathers everywhere.

So Yitzak went back to the Rabbi and complained. 'It only makes things worse,' he said.

'In that case,' said the Rabbi, 'bring in the goat to 20 join your family and the chicken.'

Yitzak was even more confused, but did as he was told. Soon the goat was running around eating everything he could see. First he ate Yitzak's bedspread, and then he started on the children's clothes. Yitzak hurried back to the Rabbi.

Illustrated by Sheila Moxley

'My house is more crowded than ever!' he cried.

'In that case bring in your cow to live with your family, the chicken and the goat.'

Yitzak couldn't understand what was going on at all, but he trusted the Rabbi's wisdom. So he went home and brought in the cow. But the huge cow immediately knocked over all the pots and pans and plates. By now the house was so crowded that no one was able to move. Yitzak rushed off once more to see the Rabbi.

'Rabbi,' he cried, 'there is no room to breathe in my house. If it stays like this we will all go mad!'

'Don't worry,' said the Rabbi. 'I have another idea. Go home and take the chicken, the goat and the cow out of the house.'

Yitzak was completely puzzled, but he did as the Rabbi had said. He put all the animals back in the yard, and then an amazing thing happened. Without the animals the house seemed as big as a mansion. There was room for all his children, his wife and himself. So Yitzak and his family learned how to appreciate what they had, and they lived happily ever after in their huge little house.

27

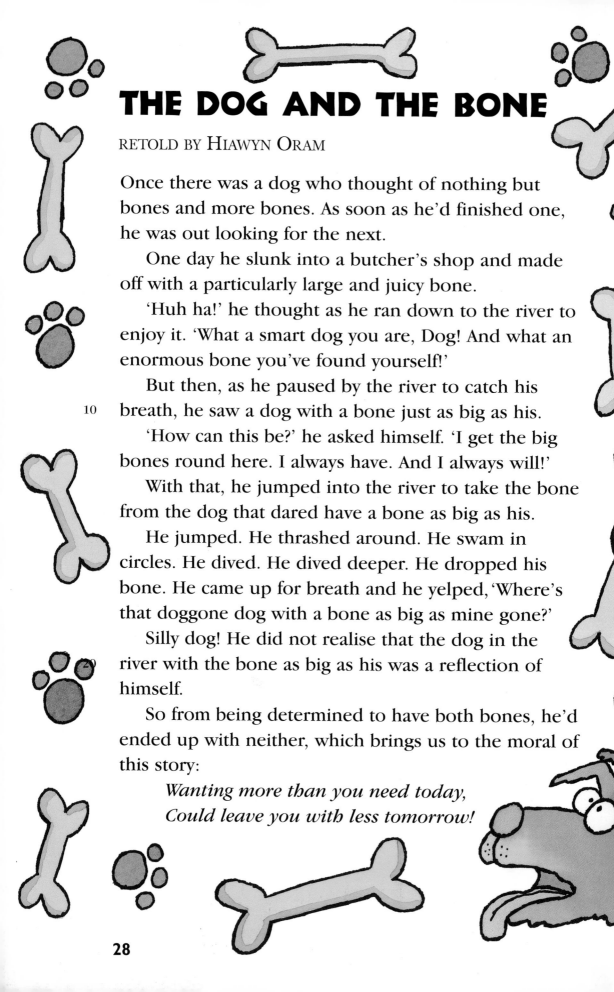

THE DOG AND THE BONE

RETOLD BY HIAWYN ORAM

Once there was a dog who thought of nothing but bones and more bones. As soon as he'd finished one, he was out looking for the next.

One day he slunk into a butcher's shop and made off with a particularly large and juicy bone.

'Huh ha!' he thought as he ran down to the river to enjoy it. 'What a smart dog you are, Dog! And what an enormous bone you've found yourself!'

But then, as he paused by the river to catch his 10 breath, he saw a dog with a bone just as big as his.

'How can this be?' he asked himself. 'I get the big bones round here. I always have. And I always will!'

With that, he jumped into the river to take the bone from the dog that dared have a bone as big as his.

He jumped. He thrashed around. He swam in circles. He dived. He dived deeper. He dropped his bone. He came up for breath and he yelped, 'Where's that doggone dog with a bone as big as mine gone?'

Silly dog! He did not realise that the dog in the 20 river with the bone as big as his was a reflection of himself.

So from being determined to have both bones, he'd ended up with neither, which brings us to the moral of this story:

Wanting more than you need today,
Could leave you with less tomorrow!

28

THE STAG AND HIS SPINDLY LEGS

RETOLD BY HIAWYN ORAM

A stag went for a drink and saw himself reflected
in the water. 'My, what magnificent antlers I
have!' he sighed.

'But dear, oh dear, those legs!'

'What's wrong with them?' said an eel.

'So long and thin! I hate my ridiculous, spindly legs.
I'd almost rather have no legs like you.'

'I doubt it,' said the eel, but before the eel could
say more the forest filled with the yapping and baying
10 of hunting hounds.

The stag took to his heels, urging his legs to move
like the wind and take him to safety. But just as he
was almost safe, his antlers caught in the branches of
a tree.

'Don't struggle,' called a bird. 'Don't move or
you'll become more tangled, the hounds will be here
and those magnificent antlers will be the death of you.'

So, though his heart was pounding and his every
instinct was to struggle, the stag took the bird's advice.
20 Immediately his antlers came loose and his legs
were able to finish their work and carry him safely
back to his wife and children.

The stag said to his family, 'I've just realised
something. The part of me I was most proud of was
nearly the death of me and the part I despised has
saved me.'

And the moral of this story is:
> *Don't judge things by how well they look,*
> *but by how well they work.*

Illustrated by Woody

If You Want To See An Alligator

If you want to see an alligator,
you must go down to the muddy slushy
end of the old Caroony River.

I know an alligator
who's living down there –
She's a-Mean. She's a-Big. She's a-Wicked.
She's a-Fierce.

Yes, if you really want to see an alligator,
you must go down to the muddy slushy
end of the old Caroony River.

Go down gently to that river and say,
'Alligator Mama
Alligator Mama
Alligator Mamaaaaaaaaaaaaa'

And up she'll rise
But don't stick around
RUN FOR YOUR LIFE!

Grace Nichols

Illustrated by Sheila Moxley

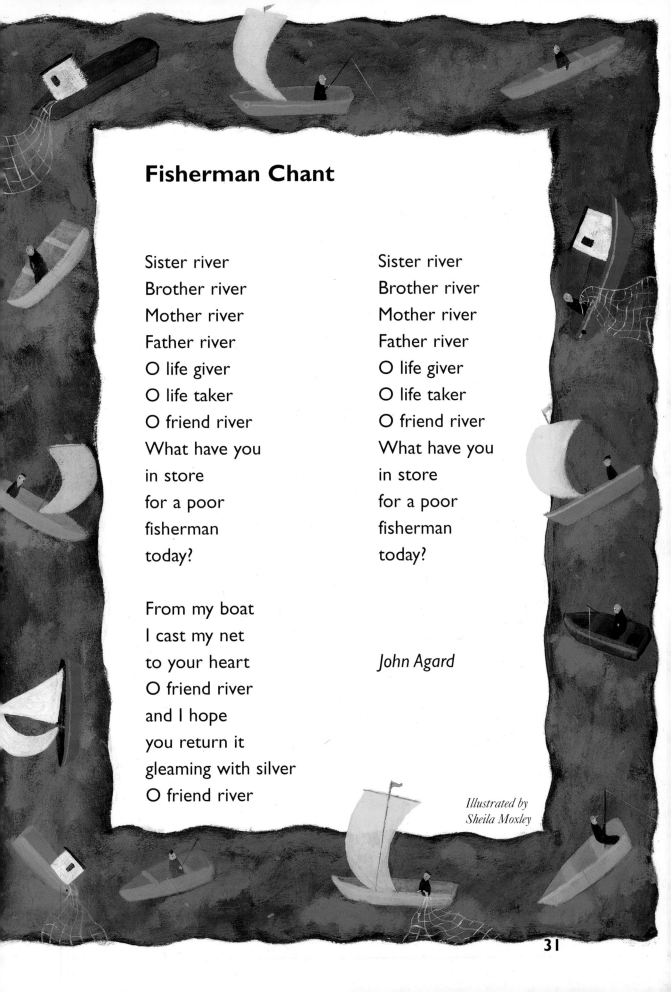

Fisherman Chant

Sister river
Brother river
Mother river
Father river
O life giver
O life taker
O friend river
What have you
in store
for a poor
fisherman
today?

From my boat
I cast my net
to your heart
O friend river
and I hope
you return it
gleaming with silver
O friend river

Sister river
Brother river
Mother river
Father river
O life giver
O life taker
O friend river
What have you
in store
for a poor
fisherman
today?

John Agard

*Illustrated by
Sheila Moxley*

Birth of the Stars

A myth from Ancient Inca

RETOLD BY JAMES RIORDAN

There was once a time when not a single star
shone in the long black night. At sunset each day, a
wizard drew a curtain across the sky, casting the
land into darkest gloom. Only at dawn did the
curtain rise to reveal the bright warm sun.

Of an evening in those distant times, people
would gather in a tent to watch as artists lit torches
and held up carved wooden figures of birds and
beasts. Then they would throw giant shadows on to
the wall of the tent, making the shadows dance and
leap about.

One day, the artists had an idea. Why not cast
their shadows on to the curtain of the sky?

So, one evening, people gathered at the foot of a
hill to watch the show. As darkness fell, the artists lit
their torches and lifted the carved figures high, so
that the shadows played upon the black curtain of
the night.

Now everyone could see the sky shadows. And
not only the people. Mice scurried into the
topmost branches of the trees. Snakes stood on
their tails to gain a better view. Even tortoises, who
had never looked above their noses, lay on their
backs to see the show.

From then on, the artists used the curtain of the sky every night as the backdrop for their show.

That is until one night, when a little moth decided to take a peep behind the wizard's curtain. Climbing up the cloth, she started nibbling a hole.
30 Just as she made a hole for her head – Flick – the wizard sent her spinning down again. But the little moth was stubborn. She flew straight back up and started nibbling once again; and she made a hole before the wizard could drive her down.

At once a little light shone through the black curtain. It was the first shining star.

The busy moth brought her friends and they made more holes. A second and a third star appeared. Soon, there were so many stars the
40 people could not count them. The whole black curtain was like a giant net with twinkling lights shining through its holes.

As the stars lit up the land, people could now see mountain paths dotted with cactus plants and eucalyptus trees. What looked ordinary by day was bathed in a magic light. They saw silver valleys, silver plains and silver streams. Yet now it was too light for the artists to perform their show.

They did not mind. After all, as people gazed up
50 at the starry sky, they were seeing the greatest picture show on earth. As for the wizard, when he saw how happy people were, he smiled and did not mind at all.

Illustrated by Tom Saecker

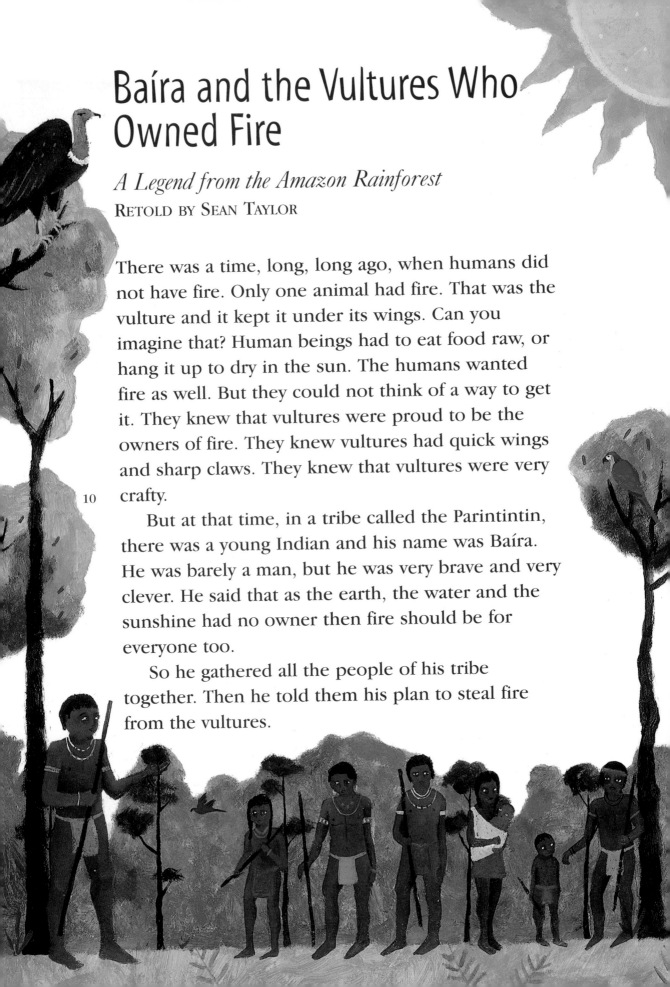

Baíra and the Vultures Who Owned Fire

A Legend from the Amazon Rainforest
RETOLD BY SEAN TAYLOR

There was a time, long, long ago, when humans did
not have fire. Only one animal had fire. That was the
vulture and it kept it under its wings. Can you
imagine that? Human beings had to eat food raw, or
hang it up to dry in the sun. The humans wanted
fire as well. But they could not think of a way to get
it. They knew that vultures were proud to be the
owners of fire. They knew vultures had quick wings
and sharp claws. They knew that vultures were very
crafty.

But at that time, in a tribe called the Parintintin,
there was a young Indian and his name was Baíra.
He was barely a man, but he was very brave and very
clever. He said that as the earth, the water and the
sunshine had no owner then fire should be for
everyone too.

So he gathered all the people of his tribe
together. Then he told them his plan to steal fire
from the vultures.

10

20　　The next day, first thing in the morning, Baíra went into the forest and covered himself in dead leaves and maggots. He lay down on the ground and there he stayed. Imagine that, lying there with maggots dancing all over you! But there he stayed, half hidden on the floor of the rainforest.

Well, after a bit he heard this ZUM ... ZUM ... ZUM. It was a blue fly. The blue fly buzzed and buzzed up above Baíra. Then it flew off. And do you know where it went? Well, I'll tell you. It went to tell the vulture
30　　that there was a dead man lying on the forest floor.

Now the vulture did not waste any time, did he?

'A dead man!' he squawked. 'Yeah, let's go!'

So he called his wife, his son, his grandmother, his wife's grandfather, his brother-in-law, his cousin, his cousin's great-grandmother and his cousin's great-grandmother's nephew and they all flew through the forest to eat the dead man lying on the forest floor.

When they got there, the vulture lifted up its wing
40　　and set fire to a stick so that they could begin to cook Baíra. A flame began to flicker brightly. Baíra opened one eye but didn't move. He waited for exactly the right moment. He waited until the stick was burning strongly. Then he sprang up, snatched it and started to run for his village.

Well! That young man he ran like the wind! He dodged between small trees! He leapt over pools of water! He ducked under vines! The vultures came flapping furiously after him. They squawked. They
50　　screeched. And they scratched at the air with their sharp claws.

Baíra tried to hide in a tree, but the vultures found him. So he ran through thick forest where the vultures could not follow.

At last he found himself at the edge of the wide river, and to get back to his village he had to cross it. How was he going to swim, holding a burning stick? The river was too wide. So he called the green river-
60 snake. He shouted:

'River-snake! Take the burning stick to the other side of the river and give fire to my tribe.'

Well, the river-snake swam with the burning stick coiled in her tail. She headed for the middle of the river, but her scales were burning – turning brown. And that's why river-snakes are brown to this day.

'Someone help!' she called. 'My scales are burning! I can't hold the fire any longer!'

So Baíra called the prawn.

70 'Prawn! Take the burning stick to the other side of the river and give fire to my tribe.'

So the prawn swam balancing the burning stick on his whiskers. He nearly got to the middle of the river, but his tail was burning – turning pink. And that is why prawns are pink to this day.

'Help! Help!' he called. 'My tail is burning! I can't hold the fire any longer!'

So Baíra called the cururu-frog.

'Cururu-frog! Take the burning stick to the other
80 side of the river and give fire to my tribe.'

So the cururu-frog swam with the burning stick in its mouth. The fire was burning its face but it was nearly across the river, so it swam on. The people from Baíra's tribe splashed into the water, took the burning stick, and held it up in the air.

Well! There was a party that night all right. The Parintintins celebrated for a whole week with songs and dances around a huge fire. And ever since that time, humans have had fire to cook their food and light their way in the night. Baíra grew up to be the great hero of his tribe.

And what about the cururu-frog? Well, because it was the one that finally got fire to the other side of the river, it became a magic animal. It became the only animal that can eat fire-flies without burning its mouth. And you know, to this day, it is still the only one that can.

Illustrated by Sheila Moxley

90

Gran, Can You Rap?

Gran was in her chair she was taking a nap
When I tapped her on the shoulder to see if she could rap.
Gran, can you rap? Can you rap? Can you, Gran?
And she opened one eye and said to me, man,
I'm the best rapping Gran this world's ever seen
I'm a tip-top, slip-slap, rap-rap queen.

And she rose from her chair in the corner of the room
And she started to rap with a bim-bam-boom,
And she rolled up her eyes and she rolled round her head
And as she rolled by this is what she said,
I'm the best rapping Gran this world's ever seen
I'm a nip-nap, yip-yap, rap-rap queen.

Then she rapped past my dad and she rapped past my mother,
She rapped past me and my little baby brother.
She rapped her arms narrow she rapped her arms wide,
She rapped through the door and she rapped outside.
She's the best rapping Gran this world's ever seen
She's a dip-drop, trip-trap, rap-rap queen.

She rapped down the garden she rapped down the street,
The neighbours all cheered and they tapped their feet.
She rapped through the traffic lights as they turned red
As she rapped round the corner this is what she said,
I'm the best rapping Gran this world's ever seen,
I'm a flip-flop, hip-hop, rap-rap queen.

She rapped down the lane she rapped up the hill,
And as she disappeared she was rapping still.
I could hear Gran's voice saying, Listen, man,
Listen to the rapping of the rap-rap Gran.
I'm the best rapping Gran this world's ever seen
I'm a –
Tip-top, slip-slap,
Nip-nap, yip-yap,
Hip-hop, trip-trap,
Touch yer cap,
Take a nap,
Happy, happy, happy, happy,
Rap-rap-queen.

Jack Ousbey

Illustrated by Tony Ross

The Travellin' Britain Rap

All the drivers rattlin' on
In a million fast cars,
Drivin' up and down the country
Like motor racin' stars,
On clearway,
Motorway,
Carriageway
And street,
Then roundabout and road
Through rain and hail and sleet,
Drivin' up and down the country
Till they're feelin' dead beat,
And the
Traffic noise,
Traffic noise
Has turned them half deaf
So they take a Welcome Break
At Happy Eater, Little Chef
And
Then
They're
Drivin' on, drivin' on
As the tyres zip and zap
Through a thousand towns and cities
That are dotted on the map
At least a million cars
– German, British, French and Jap,

never stoppin'
country hoppin'
never stoppin'
country hoppin'
For all the cars are movin'
To the travellin' Britain rap,
For all the cars are movin'
To the travellin' Britain rap,
For all the cars are movin'
To the
Travellin'
Britain
Rap!
YEAH!

Wes Magee

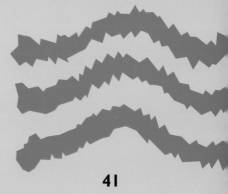

The Toad Tunnel

ANTHONY MASTERS

'STOP! TOADS CROSSING!' Jenny held up the
hand-painted sign but the cars didn't slow down at all!
They were all driving to the beach and wanted to get
to the car park before it was full.

Already, dozens of toads had been squashed flat
and Jenny was in tears. Alan and Tom watched
miserably. No one paid any attention to their sign. The
motorists obviously thought they were just messing
about.

10 'I knew this wouldn't work,' said Jenny. She looked
at Tom. 'Now you'll have to dig out that tunnel.'

'I'm not going down there,' Tom yelled. He was
sure the Giant Slime Slug lived in the tunnel. Tom had
dreamt about it last night.

In his dream, Jenny and Alan had forced Tom to
struggle through the Toad Tunnel. Halfway through, he
found that he was stuck in some horrible sticky slime.
It was like crawling through treacle.

Then Tom had heard the soft slithering of the Giant
20 Slime Slug and he saw the black monster heading
towards him. It had one eye in the middle of its
forehead and its mouth was open, showing its huge
green fangs. The Giant Slime Slug had looked very
hungry and Tom had woken up screaming.

'I'm not going down the Toad Tunnel,' he repeated.

'You've got to!' Alan was furious with him.

'It'll fall in on me,' he said miserably. 'I'll be trapped.'

'Rubbish,' said Jenny. 'It's made of concrete. It was
30 built specially for the toads to get to their breeding pool. It's just got blocked up with muck, that's all. It needs digging out and you are the only one small enough to do it. If you don't, the toads are going to keep on getting squashed!' Tom felt guilty. He should help the toads. He wanted to help the toads. But he'd always been scared of small spaces.

Alan, Jenny and Tom Sparks lived in London and were spending a weekend with
40 their grandmother in Sussex. They heard about the Toad Tunnel from her neighbour, Mr Burton. He had helped build the tunnel years ago. 'The toads always head for the breeding pool in March but they've got to get across that road. It's always been busy, so my mate and I built this tunnel under the road. The toads have been using it for years but now it's blocked with mud. Why don't
50 you three have a go at getting the muck out? I'd have a go myself if I wasn't in this wheelchair.' Then Mr Burton laughed. 'But even if I could get out and about, I'm too big.' He glanced at Alan and Jenny. 'You wouldn't get in there either. It's only young Tom who stands a chance.'

'I'm not going into that tunnel,' said Tom. 'You know I hate small spaces.'

Now Tom stood looking at the dark entrance to the tunnel. He knew he could crawl into it with his

60 seaside spade and get it clear for the toads. But what if he got trapped? What about the Giant Slime Slug?

'What about the toads?' snapped Alan. 'They're getting squashed by the minute. Are you going to let them all die?'

'You can't be so selfish!' Jenny accused Tom.

'OK,' he said miserably. 'I'll do it!'

'You'll be OK, Tom,' began Jenny more kindly. 'It won't take long.'

'Get stuck in!' Alan wasn't in the least sympathetic.

70 Tom did as he was told, and a few minutes later he had dug out quite a lot of the mud from the entrance.

'Well done!' said Jenny.

'Go for it!' encouraged Alan.

But now the worst was about to happen. He would have to get inside the tunnel.

Tom dug on, inching himself into the pipe, scraping out the mud and throwing it over his shoulder. But it wasn't the mud that he minded. It was what was waiting for him – the Giant Slime Slug.

80 Then Tom saw something glinting. Was it an eye? He froze, staring in horror at the shining thing in front of him.

'You OK?' yelled Alan. 'What are you doing?'

'Keep digging, Tom. You'll soon see daylight. It won't take long,' Jenny shouted.

But Tom couldn't hear them. He could only hear the pounding of his own heart as he stared at the winking eye.

90 He tried to back out of the tunnel but there was too much mud around him.

Then Tom felt something very light tickling his bare, muddy arm. He gave a cry of terror and saw something move. He managed to squeeze to one side and a little light shone up the tunnel.

The toad crawled away from him and then stopped, defeated by the mud wall. It crouched there, pulsating slightly, completely helpless.

Without thinking, Tom started digging again and the toad waited.

100 The eye was still there in front of them both. Then Tom's spade hit it with a clattering sound.

What an idiot he had been! Tom was gazing at a cola can which had reflected just enough light to fool him. Then, suddenly, he was out on the other side of the road.

The toad crawled out beside Tom and began to waddle down towards the breeding pond.

'Well done,' shouted Jenny and Alan. 'Well done, Tom!'

110 But all Tom could do was watch the toad until it got lost in the long grass. He was sure others would follow now that the Toad Tunnel was clear again.

Illustrated by David Kearney

How Can I?

How can I wind up my brother
when I haven't got the key?

How can I turn on my charm
when I can't even find the switch?

How can I snap at my mother
when I'm not a crocodile?

How can I stir up my sister
when I'm not even holding a spoon?

How can I pick up my feet
and not fall to the ground on my knees?

How can I stretch my legs
when they're long enough already?

Parents! – They ask the impossible!

Brian Moses

Illustrated by Nick Schon

At the End of School Assembly

Miss Sparrow's lot flew out,
Mrs Steed's lot galloped out,
Mr Bull's lot got herded out,
Mrs Bumble's lot buzzed out.

Miss Rose's class ... rose,
Mr Beetle's class ... beetled off,
Miss Storm's class thundered out,
Mrs Frisby's class whirled across the hall.

Mr Train's lot made tracks,
Miss Ferry's lot sailed off,
Mr Roller's lot got their skates on,
Mrs Street's lot got stuck halfway across.

Mr Idle's class just couldn't be bothered,
Mrs Barrow's class were wheeled out,
Miss Stretcher's class were carried out
And
Mrs Brook's class
Simply trickled away.

SIMON PITT

Illustrated by Nick Schon

A Riddle

We are invisible,
But we run your day.
We shape what you do,
And what you say.
We're often broken,
But always the same.
And we can stop anything,
Just with our name.
In one way we're nowhere,
But we're all around.
We can be made,
Remembered, or found.
Much is against us,
Because we are there;
But that's why we're needed,
Although we don't care.
We're in your classrooms,
In playgrounds, all schools.
What are we, children?
You know us, we're ...

Tony Bradman

My Dad's Amazing!

My Dad's AMAZING for he can:

make mountains out of molehills,
teach Granny to suck eggs,
make Mum's blood boil,
and then drive her up the wall.

My Dad's AMAZING for he also:

walks around with his head in the clouds,
has my sister eating out of his hand,
says he's got eyes in the back of his head
and can read me like a book.

BUT,
the most AMAZING thing of all is:

when he's caught someone red-handed
first he jumps down their throat
and then he bites their head off!

Ian Souter

Illustrated by Tony Ross

The Hodgeheg

DICK KING-SMITH

'Your Auntie Betty has copped it,' said Pa Hedgehog
to Ma.

'Oh, no!' cried Ma. 'Where?'

'Just down the road. Opposite the newsagent's.
Bad place to cross, that.'

'Everywhere's a bad place to cross nowadays,'
said Ma. 'The traffic's dreadful. Do you realise, Pa,
that's the third this year, and all on my side of the
family too. First there was Grandfather, then my
10   second cousin once removed, and now poor old
Auntie Betty…'

They were sitting in a flower-bed at their home, the garden of Number 5A of a row of semi-detached houses in a suburban street. On the other side of the road was a park, very popular with the local hedgehogs on account of the good hunting it offered. As well as worms and slugs and snails, which they could find in their own gardens, there were special attractions in the park. Mice lived

20 under the bandstand, feasting on the crumbs dropped from listeners' sandwiches; frogs dwelt in the lily pond, and in the ornamental gardens grass-snakes slithered through the shrubbery. All these creatures were regarded as great delicacies by the hedgehogs, and they could never resist the occasional night's sport in the park. But to reach it they had to cross the busy road.

'Poor old Auntie Betty,' said Ma again. 'It's a hard life and that's flat.'

30 'It's a hard death,' said Pa sourly. 'And that's flat too – talk about squashed, the poor old girl was …'

'Sssssshhhhh!' said Ma at the sound of approaching footsteps. 'Not in front of the children,' as up trotted four small figures, exact miniatures of their parents except that their spines were still greyish instead of brown. Three of them were little sows, named by Ma, who was fond of flowers, Peony, Pansy and Petunia. Pa had agreed, reluctantly, to these names, but had insisted upon his own

40 choice for the fourth, a little boar. Boys, he said, needed noble-sounding names, and the fourth youngster was therefore called Victor Maximilian St George (Max for short).

Almost from the moment his eyes had opened, while his prickles were still soft and rubbery, Max had shown promise of being a bright boy; and by now his eyes, his ears and his wits were all as sharp as his spines.

'What are you talking about, Ma?' he said.

50 'Nothing,' said Ma hastily.

'You wouldn't be talking about nothing,' said Max, 'or there wouldn't be any point in talking.'

'Don't be cheeky,' said Pa, 'and mind your own business.'

'Well, I suppose it's their business really, Pa, isn't it?' said Ma. 'Or soon will be. They're bound to go exploring outside our garden before long and we must warn them.'

'You're right,' said Pa. 'Now then, you kids, just

60 listen to me,' and he proceeded to give his children a long lecture about the problems of road safety for hedgehogs.

Max listened carefully. Then he said, 'Do humans cross the road?'

'I suppose so,' said Pa.

'But they don't get killed?'

'Don't think so,' said Pa. 'Never seen one lying in the road. Which I would have if they did.'

'Well then,' said Max, 'how do they get across

70 safely?'

'You tell me, son. You tell me,' said Pa.

'I will,' said Max. 'I will.'

Illustrated by Woody

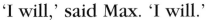

King Max The Last

DICK KING-SMITH

'THERE'S ONE!' said the man with the torch. 'Get him!'

The man with the net popped it neatly over the hurrying hedgehog. Though neither of the men could know this, they had in fact caught a most unusual hedgehog, none other than Victor Maximilian St George, known to his family as Max.

Some time ago, while trying to find a way for hedgehogs to cross busy roads in safety, Max had been hit by a passing cyclist and this had caused him to muddle his words. So that, as he told his family, 'Something bot me on the hittom, and then I headed my bang. My ache bads headly.' For some while after that, he considered himself to be a hodgeheg.

A second accident had restored Max's mind to normal, and indeed he had succeeded in his task, and had thus become something of a hero to hedgehogkind.

But now, on this particular evening, he felt anything but heroic as the net dropped over him.

He rolled himself into a tight ball, his heart hammering in fright.

54

'Stick him in this sack,' said the man with the torch.

'OK,' said the man with the net.

'He's not all that old, by the size of him. He'll do nicely.'

Max's family lived in the garden of Number 5A in
30 a row of suburban houses, and when dawn broke, they were worried.

'Ma! Pa! Our Max hasn't come home!' squeaked his three sisters, Peony, Pansy and Petunia.

'Don't fret,' said Ma Hedgehog. But she did.

'He'll turn up in a minute,' said Pa. But he didn't.

From Number 5B next door, the neighbour poked his head through the hedge. He was an elderly bachelor hedgehog, who was fond of Ma and
40 Pa's children. They called him Uncle B.

'What's up?' said Uncle B. 'Something wrong?'

'Max hasn't come home,' said Pa.

'Went across to the park last evening, hunting. He hasn't returned.'

'He probably decided to stay there and have a good day's sleep,' said Uncle B. in a comforting voice.

'But suppose ...?' said Ma, and then she stopped.

'No, no,' said Uncle B. 'Don't even think of it. If
50 there's one hedgehog in the world that knows all about road safety, it's your young Max.'

Young Max was, at that very moment, sitting in a wire cage in a laboratory at the University. The scientists who had captured him – their names were Dandy-Green and Duck – were making a study of hedgehog behaviour, and they needed to learn as much as possible of the creatures' nightlife.

'Now then,' said Dr Dandy-Green, 'we'll fit him with a radio collar.'

60 'And then we can follow his movements,' said Professor Duck.

But that was easier said than done, they found.

To begin with, when they opened the cage door and (with gloves on) lifted Max out, he rolled himself up. And even if he hadn't, they realised, fitting a collar to a hedgehog is an impossible task. For a start, a hedgehog has no neck to speak of, and anyway there's no method of getting any sort of collar to stay on, on top of all those prickles.

70 They put Max back in the cage. 'It's hopeless,' said Professor Duck. 'We might just as well let him go.'

'Not yet,' said Dr Dandy-Green. 'Maybe we'll think of something.'

So they sat and thought.

Max sat and thought too. Where was he? What was this place? Who were these men? Why had they caught him? What was to become of him? How he longed to be back at Number 5A with Ma and Pa and Peony and Pansy and Petunia and good old Uncle

80 B. next door.

Thinking of Uncle B. reminded him that the men had put a saucer of Munchimeat dog-food (the old hedgehog's favourite) in the cage. No point in starving to death, said Max to himself, and he began to tuck in.

'He's eating,' said the doctor.

'Yes,' said the professor. 'He's a nice healthy young specimen. Pity we can't make use of him.'

'You haven't thought of any way of attaching a transmitter to him?'

90 'No. Afraid not. I'm absolutely stuck.'

'Stuck?' said Dr Dandy-Green. 'Stuck! That's it!'

'What's what?' asked Professor Duck.

'That's the way to fix the transmitter. Stick it to him!'

'With superglue?'

'Yes! Stick it to the spines on the back of his head. Then we can locate him in the dark.'

'Brilliant!' said the professor. 'And I'll tell you what – we could fit him with a little flashing light.

100 Run it off the same batteries. Then we can spot him in the dark.'

'Great idea!' said the doctor

They stood up and stared into Max's cage. Max stared back.

'Wonder what he's thinking?' said Dr Dandy-Green.

'I expect,' said Professor Duck, 'that he's wishing he was back at home with his family.'

'I wish I was back at home with my family,' thought Max.

110 'He will be,' said the doctor.

'Just as soon as we've fixed him up,' said the professor. 'He's going to be a most unusual hedgehog, he is.'

Illustrated by Woody

Stranded!

ANDREW COLLETT

*When Tim and his dad find themselves
stranded in a sailing boat, all they can do is
sit and wait for the wind to gather speed. However, they
soon find that they are not alone ...*

Tim had never seen a real whale. At least, he'd never
been this close to one before. But then, he had never
been stranded at sea before.

'Don't move! Stay right where you are! It can sense
all your movements,' his dad said, trembling with fear.

At nine years of age, Tim knew all about fear. It was
the way his heart would race and his stomach would
churn if he thought he heard a noise in the middle of
the night. But he did not feel like that now. Even
though he was stranded at sea, with just his dad and a
whale for company, he was not frightened.

'It's circling us,' his dad said in a whisper, crouching
down in the hold of the small sailing boat.

Tim could see the gleaming body of the whale
pushing its way through the water just beside their
boat. He could just make out the faint bubbling of
water, like the sound of a gentle mountain stream
flowing through pebbles. And then it stopped. All at
once and without warning.

'It might have gone,' his dad said, looking up at their
limp sail. 'We'll wait a little longer. See if the wind
begins to pick up.'

Tim felt his heart start to race. Not because of the whale just to the side of them. It was certainly still there. There was something else. A dark stream-lined shape, coming towards the boat. A shark! Tim's heart beat faster. This time he really was frightened.

'There's a bit of a breeze now,' said his dad who had not yet spotted the shark. 'Come on.'

30   'No!' yelled Tim, without moving. 'Keep still!'

But it was too late. A dull thud rocked the hull followed by another… and another.

Dad saw at once what it was. 'Don't move!' he said. 'Just don't move.'

'I'm not!' shouted Tim. 'I'm not moving!'

The boat began to rock wildly from side to side. Water was spilling over the bow. The shark was attacking their boat.

Tim's stomach was churning so much that he thought
40 he was going to be sick. And as for his heart, it was
beating fast enough for it to burst right out of his chest.
He stared into his father's face. It was white – white and
full of terror.

A wave of water crashed into the boat. Tim covered
his face. And, in less time than it had taken him to blink,
his dad disappeared, swept overboard by the rush of
water.

'Dad!' Tim screamed. 'Dad!'

The thudding and banging stopped. Tim scrambled to
50 the side. The sea was still – dead still. Tim wanted to cry.
He wanted to scream. His eyes combed the still water for
life. But there was nothing – not a thing. The sea had
fallen silent. The only thing Tim could hear was his own
heart pounding inside his chest.

'Tim!' a voice suddenly yelled from behind him. 'Over
here!'

'Dad!' Tim cried.

Tim turned round and held out one hand to his
father frantically splashing about in the water. But it was
60 no good. He couldn't reach him.

'Help! Pull me up! Quick!'

'I'm trying, Dad, I'm trying!' Tim screamed helplessly.
'I'm trying.'

Then suddenly, on that last scream, a jet of water shot
high into the air. Tim stared in amazement as his dad
began to rise slowly out of the water. He was moving
upwards, almost as if he was being lifted by someone –
or something.

Tim grabbed his dad's hand. And pulled. His dad
70   tumbled into the boat. Tim fell to the floor with him.
But not before he had seen the gleaming body of the
whale sink back into the water.

'Dad! I thought ...'

'It's OK!' his dad spluttered. 'I'm OK.'

They both lay at the bottom of the boat for a few
minutes, watching the clouds gather speed above them.
A strong wind was already pulling them along. Tim
spotted something moving, and he watched as the
shark's fin quickly cut its way through the water in
80   retreat. Chased by a faint bubbling noise, like the sound
of a gentle mountain stream flowing through pebbles.

'It's going to be all right,' Tim whispered to his dad.
'It's OK.'

Illustrated by Stephen May

Through the Staffroom Door

Ten tired teachers slumped in the staffroom at playtime,
one collapsed when the coffee ran out, then there were nine.

Nine tired teachers making lists of things they hate,
one remembered playground duty, then there were eight.

Eight tired teachers thinking of holidays in Devon,
one slipped off to pack his case, then there were seven.

Seven tired teachers, weary of children's tricks,
one hid in the stock cupboard, then there were six.

Six tired teachers, under the weather, barely alive,
one gave an enormous sneeze, then there were five.

Five tired teachers gazing at the open door,
one made a quick getaway, then there were four.

Four tired teachers, faces lined with misery,
one locked herself in the ladies, then there were three.

Three tired teachers wondering what to do,
one started screaming when the bell rang, then there were two.

Two tired teachers thinking life really ought to be fun,
one was summoned to see the Head, then there was one.

One tired teacher, caught napping in the afternoon sun,
fled quickly from the staffroom, then there were none.

Brian Moses

Illustrated by Nick Sharratt

Recipe for a Disastrous Family Picnic

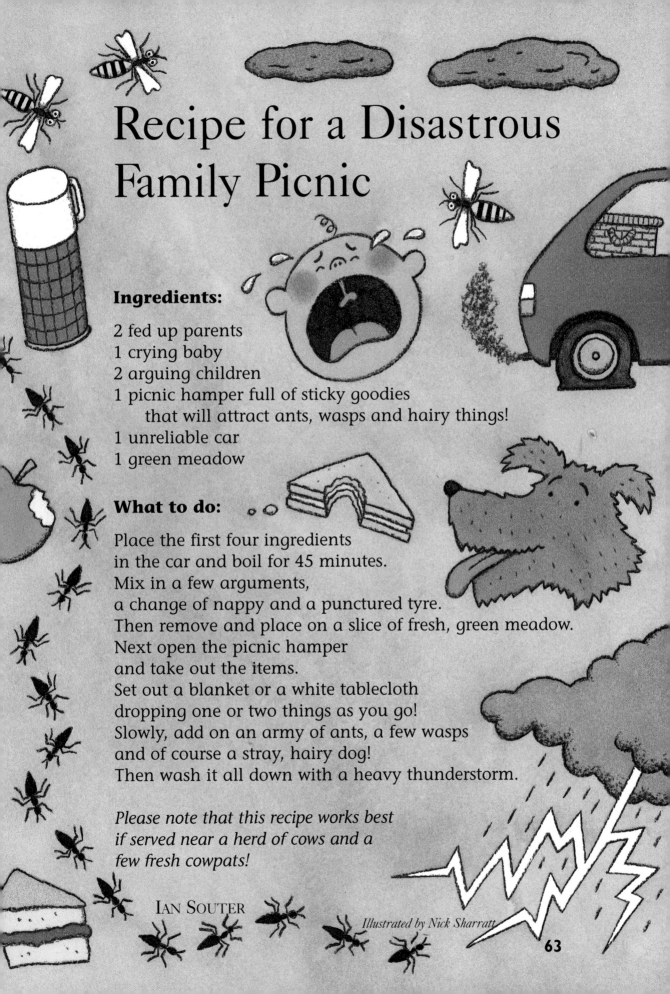

Ingredients:

2 fed up parents
1 crying baby
2 arguing children
1 picnic hamper full of sticky goodies
    that will attract ants, wasps and hairy things!
1 unreliable car
1 green meadow

What to do:

Place the first four ingredients
in the car and boil for 45 minutes.
Mix in a few arguments,
a change of nappy and a punctured tyre.
Then remove and place on a slice of fresh, green meadow.
Next open the picnic hamper
and take out the items.
Set out a blanket or a white tablecloth
dropping one or two things as you go!
Slowly, add on an army of ants, a few wasps
and of course a stray, hairy dog!
Then wash it all down with a heavy thunderstorm.

*Please note that this recipe works best
if served near a herd of cows and a
few fresh cowpats!*

IAN SOUTER

Illustrated by Nick Sharratt

Acknowledgements

The Twelfth Floor Kids by Ruth Symes, © Ruth Symes 1998

It's Not Fair!...that I'm little by Bel Mooney, from *It's Not Fair*, Mammoth 1989. Reproduced with permission of David Higham Associates on behalf of the author.

Bed in Summer by Robert Louis Stevenson

Listen by Tony Langham, © Tony Langham 1998

Rumpelstiltskin by Dee Reid. © Dee Reid 1998

The Tasting Game by Paul Stewart, © Paul Stewart 1998

The River by James Carter. Reproduced with permission of the author. © James Carter 1998

Ten Ways to Travel by Penny Kent, © Penny Kent 1998

The Gifts at the Bottom of the Well (traditional)

The Crowded House by Robert Fisher from *Together Today* © Robert Fisher 1981

The Dog and the Bone by Hiawyn Oram. © Hiawyn Oram 1998

The Stag and his Spindly Legs by Hiawyn Oram. © Hiawyn Oram 1998

If You Want To See An Alligator by Grace Nichols. Reproduced with permission of Curtis Brown Ltd, London, on behalf of Grace Nichols, © Grace Nichols 1988

Fisherman Chant by John Agard. By kind permission of John Agard, c/o Caroline Sheldon Literary Agency, from *You'll Love This Stuff*, CUP 1988

Birth of the Stars by James Riordan, © James Riordan 1998

Baíra and the Vultures Who Owned Fire by Sean Taylor. Reproduced with permission of Celia Catchpole Agency on behalf of the author, © Sean Taylor 1998

Gran, Can You Rap? by Jack Ousbey. Reproduced with permission of the author; first published in *All in the Family*, OUP 1993

The Travellin' Britain Rap by Wes Magee from *Getting in Touch with Wes*, © Wes Magee 1992

The Toad Tunnel by Anthony Masters, © Anthony Masters 1998

How Can I? by Brian Moses, © Brian Moses 1995 from *Rice, Pie and Moses*, published by Macmillan

At the End of School Assembly by Simon Pitt, from *Crack Another Yolk*, ed. John Foster

A Riddle by Tony Bradman. Reproduced with permission of The Agency on behalf of the author, from *My First has Gone Bonkers*, 1993

My Dad's Amazing! by Ian Souter, © Ian Souter 1998

The Hodgeheg by Dick King-Smith. Reproduced with permission of AP Watt on behalf of Dick King-Smith, from *The Hodgeheg*, Puffin Books 1989

King Max The Last by Dick King-Smith. Reproduced with permission of AP Watt on behalf of Fox Busters Ltd, from *King Max The Last*, Puffin Books 1996

Stranded by Andrew Collett, © Andrew Collett 1998

Through the Staffroom Door by Brian Moses, © Brian Moses 1996 from *Secret Lives of Teachers*, published by Macmillan

Recipe for a Disastrous Family Picnic by Ian Souter, © Ian Souter 1998

Every effort has been made to trace copyright holders but we would be glad to rectify any omissions at the next reprint.